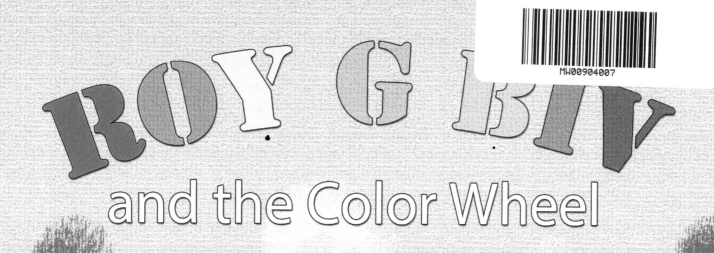

ROY G BIV

and the Color Wheel

Story by Mike Kelly
Art by Chris Malone

AuthorHouse™
1663 Liberty Drive
Bloomington, IN 47403
www.authorhouse.com
Phone: 1 (800) 839-8640

Story by Mike Kelly
Art by Chris Malone

Published by AuthorHouse 05/05/2016

ISBN: 978-1-5049-0974-7 (sc)
978-1-5049-0972-3 (hc)
978-1-5049-0973-0 (e)

Library of Congress Control Number: 2015906719

Print information available on the last page.

authorHOUSE®

Thank you

This work could not have been completed without:

Chris Malone- Illustrator
Cheri Correll- Art teacher
Adair Correll- Singer, song/music writer
Yvette M Burton- My daughter

Dedication

To the entire Kelly Clan

T. Harold Bowles Jr.
My friend-brother-mentor

ROYGBIV...... All the colors you will ever need
To plant your pallet with color seed......ROYGBIV

The color red comes from the heart....
it's sent down from above
It's warm.... it's bright.... It's so much fun
It's known as the color of Love

The color orange is energy
And we hope you are aware
When orange is on the color wheel
Energy is always there

ROYGBIV...... All the colors you will ever need
To plant your pallet with color seed......ROYGBIV

Yellow is fun...it's a big wide smile
A great big happy face
Warm and fuzzy feelings
Live in the yellow place

The color green.... is all about life
You can find it everywhere
Think in many shades of green
And life can take you there

ROYGBIV...... All the colors you will ever need
To plant your pallet with color seed......ROYGBIV

Blue is when you're peaceful
A cloud that you can share
This cloud can make you happy
Blue will take you there

Royal Violet when combined with blue
Is known as Indigo
It's very bold and vibrant
It has a power glow

ROYGBIV...... All the colors you will ever need
To plant your pallet with color seed......ROYGBIV

Red, Blue and Yellow
Primary colors ....Oh so real
Violet, green, and orange
Are secondary on the color wheel

Black is Black ....white is white
There's not much else to say
But mix the two together
They become a neutral gray

ROYGBIV...... All the colors you will ever need
To plant your pallet with color seed......ROYGBIV

Bridge:
You can paint them straight or mix them up...
You'll learn to paint with a rainbow brush....
Create paintings with a magical feel
Using all the colors on the "Color Wheel"
Create paintings with a magical feel
Using all the colors on the "Color Wheel"

FOR A SING-ALONG MUSIC VIDEO, SCAN THIS QR CODE OR VISIT
http://youtu.be/myOyqVE6cq4

ROY G BIV

EVERY COLOR

IN THE RAINBOW

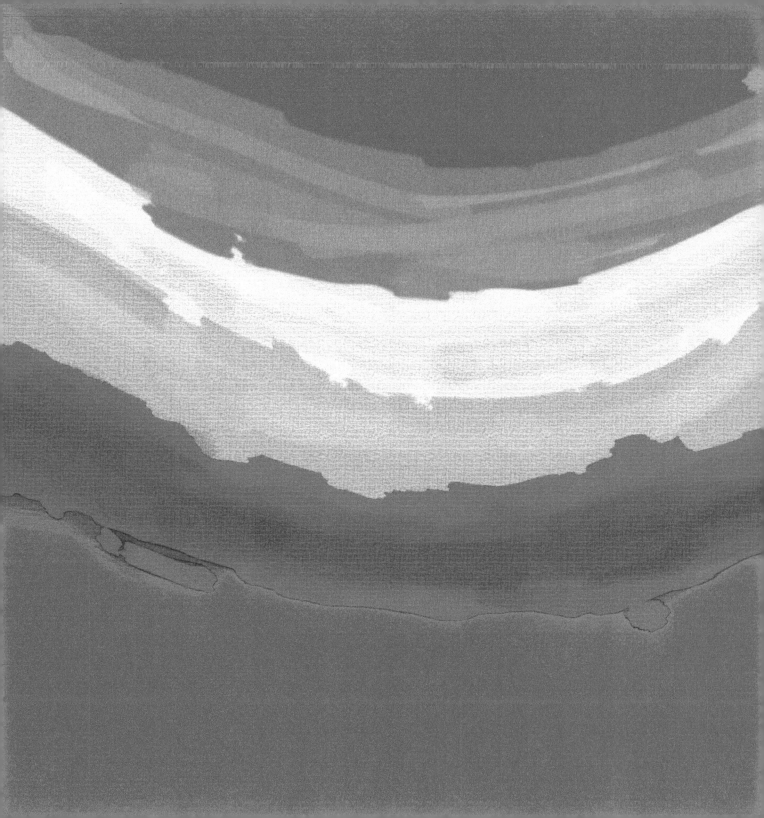

ONCE UPON A TIME THERE LIVED A VERY **COLORFUL CHARACTER ROY G BIV**

YOU COULD TELL HIS FEELINGS BY LOOKING AT HIM

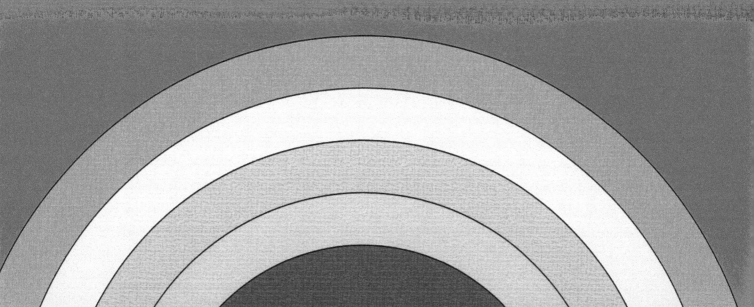

HE COULD BE

RED

FILLED WITH
LOVE

HE COULD BE

YELLOW

WITH HAPPINESS

WHAT

COLOR

IS

HAPPINESS?

yellow

WHAT

COLOR

IS

LIFE?

green

OR

BLUE

WITH

PEACE

WHAT

COLOR

IS

PEACE?

blue

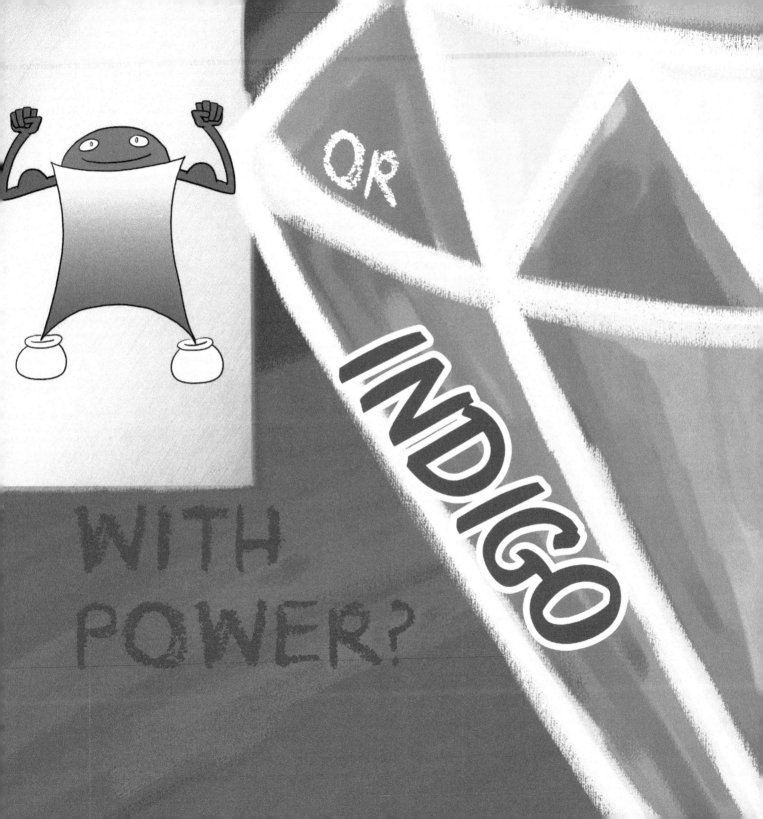

WHAT TWO COLORS MAKE INDIGO?

blue and violet

VIOLET

AND LIKELY

VIOLET

ROYALTY

WHAT
COLOR
IS
ROYALTY

violet

HIS PRIMARY MOODS

RED

BLUE

WHAT ARE THE PRIMARY COLORS?

red, yellow and blue

HIS

SECONDARY

MOODS

ORANGE

GREEN

VIOLET

THE SECONDARY COLORS ARE?

orange, green, and

ALL

THE

WAY

TO

NEUTRAL

GRAY

B	L	A	C	K
	A	N	D	
W	H	I	T	E

MAKE ??? WHAT

GRAY

GLOSSARY

R	RED		FILLED WITH LOVE
O	ORANGE		FILLED WITH ENERGY
Y	YELLOW		FILLED WITH HAPPINESS
G	GREEN		FILLED WITH LIFE
B	BLUE		FILLED WITH PEACE
I	INDIGO		FILLED WITH POWER
V	VIOLET		FILLED WITH ROYALTY

PRIMARY COLORS ARE RED YELLOW BLUE

CANNOT BE MADE FROM ANY OTHER COLOR

SECONDARY COLORS ARE ORANGE GREEN VIOLET

MADE BY MIXING TWO PRIMARY COLORS

RED+YELLOW=ORANGE

YELLOW+BLUE=GREEN

BLUE+RED=VIOLET

TEST

R	WHAT COLOR IS LOVE?		RED
O	WHAT COLOR IS ENERGY?		ORANGE
Y	WHAT COLOR IS HAPPINESS?		YELLOW
G	WHAT COLOR IS LIFE?		GREEN
B	WHAT COLOR IS PEACE?		BLUE
I	WHAT COLOR IS POWER?		INDIGO
V	WHAT COLOR IS ROYALTY?		VIOLET

PRIMARY COLORS CANNOT BE MADE FROM ANY OTHER COLOR? YES NO

ARE THE PRIMARY COLORS RED YELLOW BLUE? YES NO

SECONDARY COLORS ARE MADE BY MIXING TWO PRIMARY COLORS? YES NO

ARE THE SECONDARY COLORS ORANGE, GREEN, AND VIOLET? YES NO

IS THE COLOR ORANGE MADE BY MIXING RED+YELLOW? YES NO

IS THE COLOR GREEN MADE BY MIXING YELLOW+BLUE? YES NO

IS THE COLOR VIOLET MADE BY MIXING BLUE+RED? YES NO

Mike Kelly is the founder of Theatre North TC.
Artist, producer, director, actor, teacher.
Dedicated to teach the color wheel to children of
all ages. He already has the next 4 books
in the *Roy G Biv* series ready.
His favorite color is kelly green.

Chris "Kilika" Malone is best known for his
online comic strip, *Blue and Blond*, but he's
currently producing two new comics, *the Steele
Society*, and *the Legend of Stache*. In addition
to comics, he also does animation work on
the Emmy-nominated show, *Archer* for FX, and
Army of Frogs through Secret Sauce Studio.
He loves surfing, drawing, dogs and guinea
pigs. His favorite color is cerulean blue.